MATCHED TO PATRICK

IRIS WEST

To you, my reader. I hope you love Blossom Ford, and the sexy men, curvy women and kind but extremely interfering folk that live there, as much as I do.

1 PATRICK

MINGLED LAUGHTER DRIFTS from the sitting room, bringing mixed feelings of joy and sadness. We decorated the entire house in green–it's St Patrick's Day. As usual, we've been to church and are now having beef pot roast, which Mom and Aunt Shauna insist on making every year on the feast day of St. Patrick. Dad would have been so happy to hear that laughter. Even though we gathered like today at Christmas, St Patrick's Day was his favorite holiday.

I remove more salad from the refrigerator.

"Ready for the parade of women our moms no doubt have lined up for you this year?" My cousin Lorcan asks. I know his lilting voice like I know my own.

I snap the refrigerator closed. "Will I be the only one on display?"

He winces. "You're the eldest. And you're Aunt

1

Caitlin's only son, so you'll definitely be in the firing line. Mom will surely want to marry Riordan off first. I'll be an afterthought."

The lump in my throat prevents me from chuckling. I can't really blame Lorcan. I used to be like him. The thought of marriage drove me barmy. Not anymore.

At first I couldn't imagine myself being happy with a family, not with the crushing guilt I felt over what happened to Little Fiona. Before Dad passed, he made me promise to let go of that guilt and cherish the time I've been blessed with. Although I believed it'd never happen, little by little, I'm appreciating life.

I want what Mom and Dad had, though. They were meant for each other. Someone out there is my soulmate and the moment I find her, I'm not letting go. For the last couple of years, Mom and Aunt Shauna's matchmaking efforts haven't bothered me in the least.

I glance outside to where Riordan, my cousin and Lorcan's eldest brother, sits in the spring sun. "Riordan is not ready to get married. I doubt he'll hang around for the picnic and anyone our moms might want to set him up with."

That giant of a man is still blaming himself for what happened to his little sister Fiona, even though it's been twenty-six years since she was taken from us. Our dads were first cousins -both O'Connors. The two of us are forty-four, but I'm older than Riordan by one week. As the oldest children in the O'Connor family, it was our responsibility to make sure Fiona was safe.

Lorcan opens the back door.

"Mom is calling," he says to Rio.

It's the only thing that'll move my eldest cousin. Aunt Shauna may not be calling him now, but Riordan knows she'll soon be, wanting to make sure he spends as much time with us as possible before he scoots up the mountain.

Riordan and Lorcan's six brothers and Dad are watching TV while Mom and Aunt Shauna are chat.

"Don't forget to take good care of my friend Nara when she gets here. She was very kind to me the other day in town when I forgot my wallet," Mom reminds me.

We spend another couple of hours leisurely drinking and chatting, then get up to prepare for the outdoor picnic, which starts at four. The whole town is invited to our farm. Our parents started the tradition a few years after settling in Blossom Ford and starting a lettuce farm together, because they missed spending St Patrick's Day with their large family back in Ireland.

We put up tents on the large grass area between my house and Riordan's. Mom and Aunt Shauna used to do all the food when they were younger, but now, Lorcan gets caterers in to bring sandwiches and other finger food. By the time the townsfolk arrive, Cormac and Emmet, my youngest cousins, have set up a DJ stand which is playing upbeat music and the entire field is filled with green bunting and balloons.

I'm taking a breather from greeting people when I

see a woman strolling towards Mom. Something about the way she walks catches my attention. She's wearing black skinny jeans that mold her curvy ass to perfection and a light green top that covers a pair of generous breasts and complements the sun-kissed tone of her skin. Wavy jet-black hair falls below her shoulders and shimmers in the sun.

I'm too far away to see the color of her eyes. Before I know it, I'm marching towards Mom, curiosity and something I can't name, compelling me forward.

"I'm so glad you came, Nara," Mom is saying when I reach her side on a strategic part of the field where she, Aunt Shauna, and their friend Ms. Penny can see everyone.

Tawny, that's the color of her eyes.

I answer myself as Nara greets everyone with an amiable smile that reaches her almond-shaped, yellow-brown eyes and warms the inside of my chest. She's comfortable around Mom, Aunt Shauna and their friends, even though she must be in her mid-twenties. The silver hoops on the tops of her ears glint in the sunshine.

"This is my son, Patrick." Mom points to me.

I stretch out my hand in greeting and when she holds mine; hers is small and smooth against my large and calloused one. I don't let go and she glances up at me.

That's when I know. That I've found the woman I've spent the last few years searching for.

The friendly warmth on her face is replaced by something else: interest. A tinge of pink fills her cheeks before she pulls her hand away.

Her voice cracks a little when she says hello leaving me to wonder where the confidence she exhibited a few moments ago went.

"I'll show you where the food is," I say.

"I don't want to trouble you." She looks about her. "I'll find it, thank you."

"It's no trouble at all," Mom beams at Nara. "Patrick will walk you over to the food area. Just ask him if there's anything you need to know."

A frown forms on my face as I lead the way. At my age, I'm old enough to know when a woman has the hots for me. I know Nara fancies me, but she's decided not to pursue it.

If there's one thing I'm good at, is getting to the root of a problem. Now I've found Nara, I'll have to convince her I'm the only man for her.

2 NARA

I'VE HEARD THE expression sex on legs before, but this is the first time I've wanted to use those words to describe a man. Just looking, well, it's more like ogling really, at Patrick O'Connor's ass as he strolls to wherever the food is, is making my heart race. The heat I can feel on my cheeks has nothing to do with the eighty degrees it must be out here.

Everything about Patrick, from his wavy rich brown hair, smoldering gray eyes and over six feet athlete's body–slender yet muscular with shoulders a girl can lean on–to his easy smile that seems to invite me to trust him, speaks to the deepest part of my being.

"Thank you for helping Mom out last week. She hasn't stopped talking about you since then. You left a huge impression."

"I did what anyone would have done. It just so

happened I was the first person to witness she needed help." His mother felt unwell outside the grocery store, so I helped her get home. "Your house is beautiful."

It's a sprawling home built with solid wood.

"My dad and uncle built it. Mom and Dad were hoping to have a large family, but all God saw fit to give them was me. Even though my cousins lived just across the field, they slept over all the time, so the bedrooms weren't a waste."

"Are you talking about the other house that looks like yours but is bigger?"

"They built that too. As the family increased, they extended it."

"I'm an only child, too."

We reach three long tables piled high with food. Patrick hands me a plate.

My tummy chooses that moment to rumble. Loudly. As if it weren't enough that I'd embarrassed myself with my reaction to him in front of his mother, aunt, and their friends. I dare peek at Patrick from the corner of my eye. He's staring at me, a smile on those lips that surely belong on a woman's face. I never thought of myself as a girl who likes beards, but my fingers are itching to pet Patrick's short beard.

"Try some of Mom's food. I haven't met anyone who hasn't fallen in love with it." He places a scone and a slice of brown soda bread on my plate.

"Thank you for showing me the table. You must have guest to greet." I need to put distance between

Patrick and me. I'm too attracted to him for my own good. The more time I spend in his company, the more I find I like.

"You're Mom's special guest. I can't leave you alone. We O'Connors are very serious about paying back kindness. If I don't at least keep you company while you eat, Mom will box my ears until they are red."

The idea of Patrick being scolded by his mom is so ludicrous, a chuckle bursts from me.

"You're laughing because you've never seen Mom having a go at someone."

He touches his ear as if remembering a time it was pulled and I laugh harder.

"You're never too old to have your ears boxed at my house. Or Aunt Shauna's. She's worse than Mom, what with her redhead's temper. To be honest, I grew up with two moms, so if I ever did anything to upset Mom, Aunt Shauna would have at me. It was the same for my cousins."

It feels petty not to follow him after what he's just shared and that's how I find myself sitting cross-legged on the grass with him, a short distance away from what seems like two families with small kids.

"So, you're doing your PHD?"

I nod. I'm in food heaven. "This is fantastic. I guess I'm another person who's fallen in love with your mom's cooking."

Is he that proud of his mom's accomplishments, or is this one of his pickup lines?

Sometimes I can't believe I chose to do my doctorate in Blossom Ford instead of in Chicago where I did my undergrad and master's degree, even though my professor, the best expert in my field, moved here. Especially since the university is brand new and I'm a city girl through and through.

"What subject?"

"Biomaterials."

"I suppose you majored in something related to Materials Science and engineering or chemistry?"

"Materials Science and Engineering."

"My roommate's boyfriend was a Materials Science Major. Why did you choose to major in that?"

"Why? Because girls can't go into science or engineering?"

Patrick laughs. A couple of people nearby look over, but everyone else gets on with their conversations.

"It's impossible to believe that after growing up with Mom and Aunt Shauna," he says, when his laughter has died down. "They were eighteen when they left their home in Ireland to follow my dad and Uncle Mack here."

"Really? Both of them?"

"They've been friends since elementary school. Aunt Shauna was Uncle Mack's neighbor. She fell for the boy next door, even though he was older. Mom fell for his cousin, who used to visit regularly. When Dad and Uncle Mack left Ireland, Mom was thirteen."

"So what, your mom and aunt waited until they

were old enough and followed your dad and uncle?"

"Pretty much."

I can tell by his voice that Patrick is proud of his mom and aunt. I've always been a sucker for men who have a love of family, and Patrick clearly loves his mom and aunt. It'd be so easy to fall in love with this man.

I straighten my back. "I went into Materials Science because I want to develop affordable biomaterials that will help people. It's been a passion of mine since I was about twelve, after I saw a documentary where a little boy's wish was to have a prosthetic leg so he could run."

"A passionate choice. It suits you."

Why do I feel Patrick's not talking just about biomaterials?

Shouts have me turning toward the two families closest to us. A toddler lurches in our direction, body dangerously unsteady.

A man stands but Patrick is faster and catches her as she topples forward. He lifts her and carries her on his shoulders. The little girl chortles and waves her fists in the air.

My breath catches. My heart becomes a drum. How is it possible that Patrick looks even more gorgeous than before? He's gazing adoringly at the little girl, clear gray eyes crinkling at her as if they are sharing a private joy.

He'd make a wonderful father.

Why am I thinking about fatherhood in connection with Patrick? I place my empty paper plate on the grass.

I don't just fancy him; I'm starting to like him too. And that's dangerous. Because I'm done with falling in love with heart throbs like Patrick.

I learned my lesson when my ex, Steve, one of the most handsome boys in college, cheated on me. We dated during our last two years in college and while I did my masters. I thought our relationship was serious, but I found out later everyone but me knew he was sleeping around with other women.

A couple of years before that, I found my high school boyfriend, just as gorgeous and popular as Steve, kissing another girl. Before him I'd only had crushes, so to me, he was special.

I'm in Blossom Ford to finish my studies and that's what I'm going to do. Without distractions. I pick up Patrick's paper plate and mine and stand up. I'll have a quick chat with Patrick's mom, then leave.

3 PATRICK

IT'S BEEN TWO days since I saw Nara on Thursday, but I've been thinking about her non-stop since then. There's no doubt she's guarded against me, despite the attraction I can tell she feels for me. If Mom hadn't intervened before Mara left the picnic and offered me as a guide to show her the town, I'd have to come up with an excuse to see her. Thank God she told Mom on the day they met she hadn't taken the time to sightsee.

Even so, she politely refused my offer to pick her up. I'm in the parking lot of Blossom Ford Point waiting for her. A smile tugs at the corner of my lips. My girl is tough, and I love that about her. She needs to be to fit in with the O'Connors.

I don't know where this certainty that she's mine comes from. It's just there. This feeling doesn't care that I may have a long way to go before I can make Nara fall for me. It is just there.

I sigh. I'm not the type to give up once I've decided on something, but I hope winning Nara's heart won't take forever, otherwise I'm screwed. My hand might fall off from stroking myself to orgasm every night, thinking about her.

She pulls into the parking lot, and I watch her drive until she parks her mini beside my truck. Her hair is fastened into a ponytail. She's wearing soft pants today, but they still hug every part of her curvy legs and ass.

I tuck my hands in my pockets and after a cursory glance at her top half, decide to fix my gaze on her face. Which doesn't help because she's wearing a red-gold lipstick that makes me imagine those luscious lips on a certain part of my anatomy.

"How was your Friday?" I ask as she joins me on the path to the point. We texted yesterday to arrange our meeting, but I evaded personal conversations so I wouldn't scare her away before she has time to know me a little better.

I wonder how long she's planning to spend with me before deciding she's done time being polite and can say goodbye.

"Crazy busy. One of my experiments was successful."

She's beaming. I restrain myself from hugging her. "Congratulations. Is it a massive breakthrough?"

"Yes, and no. I have to run many more like it to get a significant result. I don't know if the next experiments will be successful."

"But you'll keep doing them?"

"God yes."

She pauses in front of the cherry tree overlooking the Ford. Wonder fills her almond eyes. "It's lovely." Her voice is hushed.

It's a beautiful day to be at the point. It's over eight-five degrees and there's no breeze. The river is tranquil and there's an air of serenity all around. But it won't last. On Sunday afternoons like this, The Point gets quite busy. A truck pulls into the parking lot. I recognize it–a bunch of kids is about to exit out of it.

"Come on. Let's go somewhere quiet and just as beautiful."

We stroll uphill past the ford and carry on marching until we reach a section where the grass is high. The area is a little wild, but it's still wonderful. Even better, it's quieter.

We sit down on an opening where the grass is beaten down in front of the river. A few cherry blossom petals float on the water.

"There's a place like this in Korea, in the town my mom is from. It's just as beautiful."

"Do you visit often?"

She shakes her head.

"My maternal grandparents didn't approve when my mother married a foreigner."

I glance at Nara. Her voice is light, but she can't hide the sadness in her eyes. I fist my hands to stop myself from hugging her.

"It must be hard for you and your family."

"It's been hardest on mom. Family is important to her. I guess she's always felt a little torn between dad and I and her parents. But now they talk to us, so it's not so bad. What about your mom and aunt? Didn't they have any grief from their parents?"

She holds up her hand to shield her face.

I rummage inside my backpack and pull out a cap. It's too big so I tighten it. "They did. For about three months. They are the type to get mad quick and make up just as quickly." I place the cap on her head.

"Thanks." She adjusts the cap before I can do it, then stands up suddenly.

"Do you know how to skip stones? I've always wondered what it was like whenever I read about it in books."

"I'm a bit of an expert."

She giggles. "Patrick, do you really get away with saying things like that?"

"You're laughing."

I must look a fool with this huge smile on my face. "But I really am one of the best among my peers. I used to do this with my cousins and friends."

She pushes her right arm back as far as it'll go and throws a stone. It falls in the water, near to where we are and sinks.

I pick a stone and throw it. She must have been counting silently because suddenly she exclaims when the bounce count passes thirty.

"Thirty-Two! That's amazing."

"It's lots of practice and a little skill."

"Can you teach me?"

There's a spark in Nara's tawny eyes that tells me she's competitive.

First, I show her how to flick her wrist. Then I correct her posture, showing her how to swing. Her skin is scalding hot when I touch her shoulder.

"Like this?" Her voice is husky.

I nod and move away from her.

She throws the stone and gets two bounces before the stone sinks. The excitement I feel at her whoop of joy only reinforces how hard I'm falling for this woman.

She tries a couple more times, then bends to pick up a stone when she trips. I catch her and gently lift her up.

I'm about to drop my hands from her shoulders when she looks up. Desire as naked as my own is reflected in her dilated pupils.

4 NARA

PATRICK'S PALMS BRAND my shoulders. I can't tear my eyes from his lips. The need to touch his beard has escalated with my feverish dreams about him, the dark look in his burning eyes and his branding touch.

Slowly, Patrick glides his thumb across my top lip, and I am undone. With a sigh, I lift on my tiptoes. I sigh again when he lowers his head. This time, it's his lips touching me.

"Nara," he murmurs hoarsely, like he's wanted to kiss me for the longest time.

I'm expecting a deep and rough kiss, but Patrick rubs his lips and nose against mine for a while first. Then he kisses each corner of my mouth. His hands rove over my back and pull me closer.

My core clenches.

"I've wanted to do this since the moment I saw you. It feels like forever."

I moan against his mouth as Patrick licks the seam between my lips.

I open my mouth, hungry to feel his tongue against mine. He angles his head and finally gives me the open-mouthed kiss I'm craving. I cup his cheeks, savoring the feel of his beard against my palms.

He thrusts his tongue against mine and I kiss him back, as deeply and hungrily as he does, until I need air and pull myself away, breathing roughly against his chest.

Patrick nips my earlobe, and my pussy clenches again. I can feel my panties getting wetter at each pull of his mouth.

"I love these," he murmurs against the hoops on the top of my ears and blows on them.

A shiver runs through me. I press small kisses against his white t-shirt, the sensation of his muscles moving under my ministrations turning me on further. My hands slide down his bearded cheeks and shoulders to his back and ass, just like in my dream last night.

A bird call breaks the silence and I'm aware of more than my thudding heart and the delicious sensations Patrick's every touch creates wherever he touches me.

I drag my hands away from his neck, and plant my feet fully on the ground, finally bringing myself to reality.

Patrick pulls back too, but his hands remain on my waist, which is hard to do considering the difference in our heights.

Air whooshes out of me when he suddenly bends down and picks me up. He sits down with me on his lap.

"Let's just stay like this for a moment, ok?" He lifts his hands then places his arms behind him, sitting back.

I watch him as he breathes in and out, his chest rising and falling under his white t-shirt fascinating me.

"I'm not interested in a casual relationship," I say when I can trust my voice. I've never been so attracted to a man as I am to Patrick. Sex with Steve was good, but this uncontrollable desire that I'm feeling for Patrick has taken me totally by surprise and if I'm honest, it's scaring me.

It's true work was brilliant yesterday, but my day was also filled with way too many moments of thinking about the dangerously hot man beside me. He should come with a warning. Don't approach if you are the type that falls hopelessly and totally in love with a man. Because that's me. My heart only seems to know how to give itself completely.

"Neither am I." He's still leaning back, but there's a solemnity about his face that moves me.

I can't think when he's looking at me like that. I get off his lap and this time he doesn't stop me.

I stare out at the river, willing my heart to be as tranquil as the surface of the water.

Patrick comes and stands beside me. Turns me toward him, then thrusts his hands into his pockets, as if he's stopping himself from touching me. "With you,

I want forever."

I shake my head. Why does everything he say sound real? His gaze is so intense, I feel like to him, I'm the only woman on earth. That I'm all he sees.

"The first time I saw your pert ass strutting towards Mom, I felt you were special. When I held your hand, I knew you were the woman I'm meant to spend my life with."

"Patrick." Words fail me. My heart is singing. The treacherous organ is already falling and believes every word.

Remember Steve and your high school boyfriend.

"Nara."

Even the way my name sounds on Patrick's lips has me wavering. "I admit I'm head over heels in lust with you. But I've never been able to get intimate with a guy without my feelings being involved. I've been hurt before, so I just want to finish my doctorate and get back to Chicago. I'm a city girl."

Patrick says nothing for a while, but his eyes remain on me. When he speaks, it's in that steady, firm voice of his, like he's just considered all possibilities and is taking this one path.

"Give me a chance to show you we're meant for each other. I know you can be happy here with me. Your passion for your work is one thing I love about you. I'll always support you."

My heart is already saying yes. I stare at the fists inside the pockets of Patrick's blue jeans; at the steadiness of his eyes as he gazes at me. I think about the way he picked up the toddler and the loving gaze with which he looks at his mom, and there's only one answer I can give him.

5 PATRICK

I WAVE TO the last of our contract workers at the end of a hot, busy day. We've been planting all day. I used to sit by the field at the end of a day like this, drinking iced beer, but the last couple of weeks I've been eager to get away and see Nara. I pinch myself sometimes because I can't believe Nara said yes that day on Blossom Ford Point. She asked me to take things slow, but I'm okay with that as long as I can spend time with her.

As I'm about to get into my truck, I spot Lorcan. He could have waited for me at home, but although he insists he's a businessman, he loves being out here.

"How did the meeting go?" I ask when he gets out of his truck.

Since Lorcan took over the finances, O'Connor Premium farm has grown exponentially. We increased our farming land from two acres to three, which has

25

allowed us to supply the lettuce we grow all over the country and across to Canada.

My agricultural degree and passion for finding innovative systems to farm ensure our production is efficient and our lettuce is the best quality in the world. However, Logan's MBA and passion for all things business safeguard our family company's outstanding profitability margin.

"We have another restaurant chain as a customer. They were so impressed with the way you run the operation. I know you accepted to lecture at the university because you want to share your experience in farming, but the lectures are a brilliant selling card for us."

I frown at the excitement in Lorcan's eyes.

"We can't take any more clients," I remind him.

"We would if we bought more land. We could also use the spare land on our property. It's just sitting here. I know our dads kept it in the hope we'd all build and settle here, but apart from the two of us, it doesn't seem like anyone is interested."

I pat his back and head for my truck. Uncle Mack is against the idea of expanding the business farther. It took a hell of a lot to convince him to buy our third acre five years ago. I agree with him. Although we hire staff and every O'Connor does their part, especially during harvest, the farm still takes a lot of our time, which means less family time.

"Are you going to see Nara?" Lorcan throws at me

as I shut the truck door.

"Jealous?"

Lorcan's flipped finger comes up in the side mirror as I drive off.

In the two-bedroom house Dad, Uncle Mack and my cousins helped me build, I shower and dress quickly. I get to Nara's apartment at the time we agreed to meet.

She's stunning in three-inch sandals, the black jeans she wore the day we met and an off the shoulder red top that is going to torture me all evening. So is the long necklace between her voluptuous breasts.

I open the passenger door and watch her stride toward me. Her quick peck is not enough to satisfy me, so I stop her from getting out of my embrace and kiss her deeply. We're both breathing hard when I pull away.

"It's still daylight!" she admonishes.

Someone shouts from one apartment for us to get a room.

Nara dashes into the truck, cheeks flaming.

I laugh. I love this side of Nara. In a highly intelligent, capable and confident young woman, the shyness she feels about public displays of affection that involve more than holding hands is highly endearing.

We talk about our day in the fifteen minutes it takes to drive from her postgrad apartment at the edge of town, near the university, to Jackson's Diner. I want to take her somewhere fancier, but tomorrow is Friday, and she runs a tutorial first thing in the morning as part of her teaching assistant duties; I have to drop her off early.

"I wish I'd tried this place earlier. I love the old family vibe it has," Nara says after Rosie leads us to a table and takes Nara's order.

"I can't imagine the waitresses at home remembering everyone's orders the way Rosie remembers yours. It'd be a nightmare."

"I went to school with her kids, so she'll always be Mrs. Lloyd to me. I don't dare call her anything else."

Nara laughs. The more time we spend together, the more she laughs. I don't know if she realizes it, but now she's not cooped up in the lab or her apartment experimenting or poring over research papers evenings and weekends, she's adapting to Blossom Ford well.

"Your mom will hear of it and box your ears," she says.

"You're getting to know how our small-town works."

"It must be hard seeing all these college students and apartments. We must have disrupted the town."

"There was definitely some vehement opposition. But a lot of young people move out of the area. The College brought in much needed business, and it's built far enough from the main part of town that it doesn't impact most of our day-to-day life. I wouldn't have you if it weren't for the university."

Our food arrives. I pick up my fork and look at

Nara's plate, then freeze.

"What's the matter? Patrick?"

The alarm in Nara's voice gets to me. I blink.

"Are you okay?" She asks.

"My cousin Fiona loved that dish. She would take out the pickles and arrange them and the burger like you did. She used to call it Mickey Mouse's head," I smile at the memory. "She was ten, with red hair and green eyes, just like Aunt Shauna. She run out onto the road to save a stray dog and was involved in a collision."

Nara lays her hand on mine and squeezes it, listening. I tell her about how losing Fiona shook our family to its core.

"I'm forgetting things about her and although that's supposed to be a good thing, it saddens me. But now I'm able to think about her without feeling like my insides are being torn apart."

"Do you hold a memorial service for her?"

"We go to mass every year on the anniversary of her passing and lay flowers on the road for her."

"I'd like to come to the next one."

My heart sings. Just like she doesn't realize she's falling in love with the town, she's not aware of how much her feelings for me have grown.

I've been careful to give her time and have taken things slowly, the way she asked me to. It kills me to take her out and return her home. Light making out isn't cutting it anymore. Every day I wake up hard with wanting her.

29

I want to see her sleeping and eating breakfast beside me every day.

My intuition is telling me it won't be long before that happens.

6 NARA

I'M STRUGGLING OUT of my car in the campus parking lot, trying to avoid hitting the car beside mine when I hear Patrick's name.

"Patrick O'Connor, you what! You got another girl? You betrayed me? I'm heading out to the farm right now," a woman shouts into her phone. She's standing by the car on the other side of mine. She's as beautiful as the models I see on TV and must be in her early thirties. While I stand outside my car, she flicks her long blond hair, enters her car and backs out.

I come to my senses when someone honks their car nearby. I get through my tutorial on autopilot and am grateful that the class only has a few undergrad students.

After the tutorial, I head to the lab. I greet the other PHD students there and sit at my desk.

I know calling Patrick is the right thing to do, but

I'm terrified he'll confirm he's dating that woman or worse, he'll deny everything only for me to find out later that it was true all along. That's what Steve did when I confronted him after I heard he was sleeping with other women. We'd been together for three years, so even though he didn't seem to be as much into me as he was when we first started dating, I believed his side of the story over rumors because we'd been together for a while, and I thought he loved me.

"Are you okay?" My friend Steph asks.

I realize I've been staring at the same paper for a while now.

"Don't you have a date?" Steph asks.

I glance at the clock. It's half-past six. "I'm leaving soon."

Steph waves goodbye. I realize everyone else has left. Sitting at my desk won't solve anything. I call Patrick.

"Hi Honey. I'm on my way to you," he says when he picks up.

Hearing the warmth and longing in his voice makes me realize I'm already in love with him. I don't want us to end.

"I'm sorry I can't make our date tonight. Can we meet at the coffee shop on campus?"

"What's the matter? Are you okay?"

"I'm fine. See you soon."

I walk over to try to clear my head. Inside the coffee shop, I see Patrick head over to a table, two cups in his hands. As if aware of my presence, he turns in my direction and watches me walk to him, his gray eyes roving over my whole body. His concern for me is palpable.

"What's the matter?" He asks once we're sitting down.

"Are you seeing someone else?" I blurt out.

His face is a study in confusion.

"No," he finally says. "I dated other women before you, I won't deny that, but you're the last woman I'll ever be with."

Maybe what I heard was about another Patrick. Yet, how many Patrick O'Connors who were farmers could there be in Blossom Ford?

"What is it? Tell me."

Haltingly, I do.

He bursts out laughing.

Tears prick my eyes.

Patrick dashes to my side of the table. He hugs me and kisses my hair.

"Silly lass," he says. He pulls out his phone. Presses a few keys, then shows me the screen. "Is this the woman?"

I stare at the picture. It's definitely the woman I saw earlier. She's wearing a wedding dress and is kissing a man who looks like a groom, but there's no mistaking it's her.

Patrick keeps the phone on the table and swipes the screen until another wedding photo appears. This time, all the O'Connors are there around the woman and what looks like her husband.

"This is Lily, who's like a sister to me and my cousins. She was Fiona's best friend. She calls me her man because I was her first crush - she was nine at the time." Patrick shakes his head, obviously still amused.

"She's happily married with kids. She's been away on vacation for the last couple of weeks and returned recently. The conversation you overheard must have been me telling her about you."

I'm so embarrassed, I don't know what to do. I close my eyes.

"I'm so sorry Patrick," I say when I work up the courage to open them.

He puts his arm around me. "I'm sorry I laughed. The idea of me and Lily together was ridiculous, I couldn't help it." His thumb strokes my nape. "If we ever come across the man who hurt you, point him out. I'll punch him for you."

A lump forms in my throat. "He's not worth it," I whisper.

"Have a look at this. It'll make you feel better." He shows me a cute video of Lily, her husband and a bunch of kids dancing. It's hilarious and gets me laughing. "I'm their uncle. You'll get a few nephews and nieces when you marry me."

I take a deep breath. This man is so open and intense. He's exactly what I need.

"Okay?"

He's still petting my nape. What should be a comforting gesture turns into something else because I suddenly can't wait to make love to Patrick.

"Do you want to go to my place?" I ask.

7 PATRICK

I DON'T LET go of Nara's hand the entire drive to her apartment, even when I park. I don't care that the elevator is packed, but Nara does so I restrain myself to holding hands. As soon as we're inside her apartment, I kiss her.

She tugs up my t-shirt but has trouble lifting it past my shoulders. I remove it in one go, drop it, not caring where it falls.

She puts her mouth on my chest and I close my eyes, enjoying the sensation of her lips moving against my skin.

"I love kissing you here, Patrick."

Me too.

"I want to see you, honey."

She undresses, her eyes on mine the whole time, unapologetically showing me all of her. Her gaze turns me on so much that even before I look at her body, my cock is straining against my trousers. When I finally see all of her, her beauty takes my breath away.

Her breasts are large, with brown nipples jutting forward, as if begging for my attention. Her skin is soft and inviting. I stare at the black curls at the juncture of her thighs and the thought of running my fingers through them causes pre-cum to seep from my cock.

"I am so glad you're my woman."

I want Nara to always smile the way she's doing right now.

I pull my pants and boxers down in one go then stalk towards her, letting her see all of me like she did.

Pink suffuses the whole of her body. I lift her and her legs wrap around my waist.

I've only been to her place once, but I remember the way to the bedroom.

Nara kisses me and threads her hands through my hair.

In the bedroom, I place her on the bed.

"I've imagined our first time together so many times. I'm going to kiss every part of you, even if it kills me."

I kiss her forehead, eyes, pert nose, and lips. I nip her ear lobes and graze the skin around her earrings.

She moans. I take her mouth again, swallowing the noises she's making. I trail kisses along her collarbone. My hands move to her breasts and circle them. They feel just right in my hands. I squeeze them and run my thumbs across her nipples.

Nara whimpers. I lick one hard point until it feels like a pebble. Then I take it into my mouth, sucking on it like it's candy.

"Patrick, that feels great." Her voice is raw with desire.

I transfer my mouth to her other breast and once again lick the nipple until it's stone hard before sucking it.

I kiss my way down her tummy to her belly button and swirl my tongue there, exploring the silver hoop adorning it. It's quickly becoming one of my favorite places on Nara's body.

I rub my nose against the curls on her mound, then run my calloused fingers through them.

Her engorged clit is a work of art.

I take a deep breath before stroking it. I'm so hard, I'm afraid touching her might be the end of me. But I swore to myself the first time we made love; I'd treat her like a queen.

I touch her gently at first, learning what she likes. She fists the sheets and lifts her hips. I flick my tongue repeatedly over her clit and insert a finger into her dripping pussy. She's so slippery that I add another two digits and finger fuck her until she arches off the bed in pleasure.

"Aw Nara, you taste so good." I kiss her so she'll know how wonderful she tastes.

Grabbing her curvy ass with both my hands, I pause with my hard cock over her pussy.

I groan when Nara fists me and guides me towards her core.

I penetrate her in one plunge. Even though she's soaking wet, she's tight. I groan again, desperately trying to resist the desire to pound into her.

Nara winds her legs around my waist. I want to see her orgasm again, so I fuck her slowly until her fingers rake over my back and dig into my ass.

I increase my pace and thrust furiously into her sweet heat. I reach between us and stroke her clit until she screams my name, the contractions of her pussy strangling and catapulting me into the best orgasm I've ever had.

Spent, I roll onto my back, pulling her against me.

"I love you, Patrick."

"Aw, honey, I love you too."

I interlace our hands and lift them up. Then I look at the woman who's brought so much joy into my life.

"Nara Johnson, will you marry me? You complete my life, and I want to spend the rest of it with you. I promise to always support your dreams."

Her yellow-brown eyes widen. Then she smiles. "I love the way you love me, Patrick. I can't wait to spend my life with you."

I kiss her forehead. Then I think of something and my heart sinks.

"Did you want a big proposal?"

"No. This is the perfect proposal. You're perfect for me, Patrick O'Connor."

EPILOGUE - NARA

One Year Later – St Patrick's Day

"YOU HAVE A baby girl, Mr. and Mrs. O'Connor," the midwife says.

She places our daughter in Patrick's arms.

I've never seen him so dumbstruck. He blinks and I know him well enough to realize he's hiding tears. He walks over to me and places our little girl in my arms.

"She's gorgeous," he whispers. "Thank you, honey."

I look at our little bundle. Patrick is right. She's a beauty.

"Are you sure about her name?" he asks.

"I'm surer than before she was born. The name suits her."

"Hello Fiona," Patrick croons to his daughter, petting her cheek with the knuckles of one hand.

I surprised myself by not wanting to find out the sex

of the baby. I'd always thought of myself as a rational person, and it made sense to know if we were having a boy or girl so we could plan. But I wasn't bothered. Neither was Patrick. We decided if the baby were a girl, I'd name it and if it were a boy, he would be in charge of naming.

I chose Fiona.

I've discovered so many things about myself since I married Patrick only two and a half months after he proposed. The only person who wasn't surprised when I accepted to marry him after a short proposal was Patrick.

"They don't know how well I treat you," he'd said when I told him my folks were surprised I'd agreed to a quick wedding.

He still treats me well. A little too well sometimes. All the O'Connor men do. I had to be very assertive not to be waited upon like an invalid from the time I discovered I was pregnant. If they had their way, I wouldn't have been able to carry on working until two weeks before my due date or do any housework and cooking.

My brilliant PHD supervisor, whose expertise in biomaterials is the reason I'm doing my PHD in Blossom Ford, was taken aback when I announced my marriage and later pregnancy but was supportive once he got over the shock. I worked so hard before dating Patrick; I was well ahead of schedule. Seeing me work almost as hard as before my pregnancy did a lot to reassure him I was still committed to our research.

I learned to leave my work at the office, though. My evenings and weekends were for family. Looking at Fiona, I'm glad I got used to doing that before she came along, as it'll come in handy when my little girl is a year old, and I return to work.

Patrick and I are lucky his mother and aunt come over to our place to help with cooking and cleaning. They can't wait to babysit too.

As soon as the midwifes finish tidying up the room and leave, a knock sounds on the door. I'm bombarded with well wishes from the entire O'Connor clan and my parents. Despite Patrick reminding everyone to be quiet, I'm sure they are going to be kicked out soon. There are just too many of them packed into the hospital room.

They all treat me like a little sister (even Cormac and Emmet, who I repeatedly call by the wrong name because they're identical twins) or a daughter. I feel I gained eight brothers, two moms and a dad instead of in-laws.

Mom and Dad were worried about the nineteen years between Patrick and me at first, but once they got to know him, they supported our relationship unreservedly.

"Are you tired? Shall we kick everyone out?" Patrick whispers.

"I love seeing our family like this. And it's St Patrick's Day. They'll leave soon to get ready for the picnic."

"God, I love you, Nara O'Connor."

The End

MARRYING THE PROTECTIVE PROFESSOR

CURVY BRIDES OF BLOSSOM FORD #1

1 AUGUST

ALL MY LIFE I've secretly wished I was born and raised in an ordinary family, with loving, welcoming parents instead of being the town's sign of bad luck, growing up at Blossom Ford Orphanage and having the town's name as my surname, like the other kids there. I can't help believing if I was wanted, the acceptance and sense of belonging would have helped me become someone who knows how to love. That belief is strongest when I think of Ella Mitchell.

It's Friday night so ensuring she gets home safely is my top priority as I park my SUV a short distance from Jackson's Diner where she's working, far enough to see the door of the restaurant but not so close that anyone might link my presence to the diner. I don't care how the interfering residents of Blossom Ford view me, but I don't want rumors to spread about Ella.

I slide down the car seat, getting comfortable even as I curse myself for the warmth that spreads through my chest at the mere thought of her name. As I've done a millionth time, I tell myself I'm here to protect her.

An uncomfortable tightness in my chest and a bitter taste in my mouth that I'm all too familiar with have me exhaling slowly. But it's hard to chase away the guilt. I cannot keep from committing the same sin. I'm a scarred, divorced, grizzly mountain of a man that's old enough to be her father while she's a beautiful, innocent twenty-two-year-old with her whole life ahead of her. Ella deserves better than me. But I still can't stop thinking about her.

It makes no difference that what I feel for her is more than physical attraction. I love her strength, soft smile and the way she's warm to everyone that crosses paths with her. There's a certainty in my bones that she's meant for me alone. This only makes the guilt worse. I should let her go because I love her.

And I have. To a point. For the last two years since I returned to Blossom Ford, saw her for the first time and fell for the kindness in her honey hued eyes and the sweetest curves I'd ever seen, I've stopped myself from approaching her. From claiming her. At least in real life. Because in my dreams, I've made love to her every single night and spent my days laughing with her. I've always considered my self-control one of my strongest attributes, but I can't stop dreaming about her.

I can't help the fact that I won't have her driving home by herself at midnight, after her shifts at the diner on Fridays and Saturdays. If I'm an asshole, so be it. And if deep down I know as well as ensuring she's safe, I have to see her face, I'll take the guilt and deal with it.

I frown when only two cars remain in the parking lot. One is old Jackson's beat up truck, and the other belongs to Rosie; the woman who works with Ella. Ella's old yellow mini should be right besides Rosie's.

The door to the diner flies open and Rosie marches out in her apron, phone glued to her ear. She sprints to her car. My frown thickens. How is Ella going to get home? Will she be closing on her own? I force myself to stay in the car. As much as I want to rush in and help, keeping a distance is crucial to my self-discipline.

I ramp up the air conditioning in the car a little higher. It usually takes one hour to close, but tonight, it'll take Ella longer. Old Jackson doesn't think hard work hurts women. There's no way he's going to help with setting the dinner to the way he likes it.

I keep my eyes on the door and an hour and a half later, I'm rewarded with the sight of Ella's curvy hips wrapped in hugging denim and the soft way her breasts hug her blouse. Even after a ten-hour shift, she's a vision that gets my heart racing.

She zeroes in on my car and it's like she can see me,

like she knows I'm waiting here for her. She does this on Fridays and Saturdays; the days I wait for her. If she worked any other nights, I'd wait for her then, too. She's friends with Mrs. Gallagher, the orphanage director who's the closest thing to a mother I've ever had. Ella must think of me as a much older brother who's looking out for her.

She steps on the street and heads towards me. I know that she's just taking the road to her house, but I can't stop my heart from beating even faster. It's like this every time I see her.

I'm feeling something else too; anger. Her walking alone down the empty street at this time of the night is pissing me off.

She's only a few feet from me when a car careens down the street and stops beside her. I sit up straight, hoping a friend is coming to pick her up. But she doesn't slow down, even after spotting the car.

I scowl as a man stumbles out of the car and steps in her path. It's Toby Anderson, Ella's ex. Something ugly rears in me. Despite my unstoppable feelings for Ella, whenever I see him, I realize how great my self-control is. Every time I saw him with Ella, I wanted to knock him out. The four months they dated were an exercise in self-discipline I didn't think I was going to win. But for Ella, to give her the chance at happiness she deserved with someone her age that could give her a comfortable life, I held myself back.

I don't like the way Toby sways on his feet. The light

from the full moon and lamppost in front of the diner are enough to make out the disgust on Ella's face. Before I know it, my hand is on the door handle, but my eyes don't stray from Toby.

They are talking but the loud music and shouts from the car stop me from hearing what they are saying. Toby reaches out a hand and touches Ella's arm. She wrenches it back.

I'm out of the car. i sprint towards them, her safety the only thought in my mind. for her, I'd tried staying away, but her safety is something I'll not compromise on. even if it means she might hate me for interfering with her life.

MARRYING THE BROKEN BOSS

CURVY BRIDES OF BLOSSOM FORD #2

1 TIANA

I RUN AS soon as the bus door opens. I hate being late. My number one rule is Do Not Be Late. Even though I know better, I ask myself why the bus had to be late today of all days when I usually can tell the time by Blossom Ford busses.

A car is coming in the opposite direction, but I figure I have enough time to cross the street. I dash across, avoiding a big puddle of water on the side of the road, but a couple of steps onto the pavement, a cold rush stops me. I glance at my front and side. They are both wet and so is part of my face and hair.

I turn around, but the car is already roaring off in the distance. A string of curses comes out of me before

I can stop it. Now I'm late and messy. Even the image of Mum standing with her hands on her hips, saying she's gonna wash my mouth with soap, doesn't stop the cuss words. I set off again and sigh when I spot the humongous old house with a wrap-around porch.

I push the bell at the large gate, the butterflies that started dancing earlier this morning doing acrobatics with the added worry of my lateness and visual. I don't want my patient to think I'm a rag doll when they meet for the first time. Not patient, I correct myself, client. And a filthy rich one at that. If he takes me on as his physical therapist, he'll be my boss for the foreseeable future.

"Yes?" The voice is terse over the intercom.

"It's Tiana Remington, the physical therapist."

The intercom buzzes, and the gate swings open when I push it. I race up the long drive, fisting my free hand. I worked hard during my training period and the following years at a rehab center to know I'm very good at what I do. But this is only my second private gig, and the agency warned me to make sure I'm extra professional with Mr. cooper. There's nothing I can do about the tardiness but I have to do something about my appearance.

Near the front door, I whisk out a mirror and peer at my face and head. I get tissues from my bag and dab wet skin and hair, glad my eye liner only ran a little. There's no time to retouch my make-up. The tissue is only leaving white bits on my clothes, so I give up. I say a prayer of thanks that my top is dark blue and my trousers are even darker, then tell myself to stow away my mirror.

"Is checking your make-up when you're late part of the professionalism you mentioned in your resume?"

I gulp, feeling like a kid caught red-handedly shoving a hand into the cookie jar. I stare in the voice's direction and my breath catches. It's been a long time since I've seen such an amazing posture. A chest that makes me think the man at the door of the house must work out daily offsets straight back and square shoulders, even though he's in a wheelchair. He has green eyes, dark brown hair and a beard I want to pet. I realize I'm staring and clear my throat.

"Mr. Cooper?" Where's my usually calm voice?

"Let's get started, shall we?"

Breathe, I tell myself. I am a professional. I'm good at my job. Being turned on by a man's great posture doesn't make me weird. It's normal, cause I'm human. Also, I will not crush on my boss, I recite as I hurriedly close the distance to the door and get in the house just in time to see Mr. Cooper enter a room off the hallway.

I close the door and walk to the room. As I walk in, he doesn't take his eyes off me. Shaping my lips into my most professional smile, which makes the grumpiest of patients smile back, I hold out my hand.

"We've lost enough time. Let's begin."

I just about keep the smile in place and sit in the chair facing him, putting my bag on the floor. He's mad, I get it. I'd be mad too if I'd been as late as I am, but his rudeness is disconcerting.

"If you can't get here in time, why should I have you as my physical therapist?"

I purse my lips to stop the explanation of how I'd actually left extra early to ensure I got here early, but the bus had broken down and the next one had been late too. There was an air about Caleb Cooper that screamed of confidence, strength and self-discipline. He wouldn't care about excuses.

I look at him and make my voice strong. "I want to open a private practice by the time I'm 30. Being financially stable is crucial to me. As you will have heard from the client that recommended me, I know what I'm doing. I'm very discreet and am willing and able to carry out any other housekeeping or administrative tasks you may require. I believe those are the requisites you're looking for. There was an unavoidable circumstance today. I apologize; it won't happen again." Heartbreak over Mum and Dad's rows about money before their bitter divorce taught me the importance of money.

He searches my face for a while, then nods and interlaces his fingers over his knees.

Inside, I do a little dance of gratitude as I take out my tablet and find the files his doctor and previous physical therapist sent. I studied them last night, so I just need to ask a few questions and take down any new information before we come up with a treatment plan that'll work for him.

"What do you think is the biggest challenge to your mobility now?" I ask and discover it's not just his posture I like. He answers my questions and asks his own with knowledge that shows he's done a great deal of research about his spinal cord injury.

OTHER BOOKS BY THE AUTHOR

MARRYING THE PROTECTIVE PROFESSOR

MARRYING THE BROKEN BOSS

MARRYING THE GRUMPY DIRECTOR

MARRYING THE POSSESSIVE NEIGHBOR

MARRYING THE WIDOWED DOCTOR

MARRYING THE SCARRED SOLDIER

MARRYING THE OBSESSIVE CEO

MARRYING THE BIG MOUNTAIN MAN

ABOUT THE AUTHOR

Iris West writes short and spicy romance about alpha heroes and the women they can't help falling in love with. She loves reading all types of romance books that have a happy ending and is an avid Kdrama fan.

Follow or like her on Facebook, Goodreads.

FREE BOOK

Would you like a free book? Sign up to my mailing list at https://dl.bookfunnel.com/t191w45ryj to receive a copy of Loving My Fake Husband, a free to subscribers only, Curvy Brides of Blossom Ford Series short story.

HELP OTHERS FIND THIS BOOK

Thank you for reading Marrying The Protective Professor. If you enjoyed this book, please help others discover it by leaving a review at your favorite online book store.

Many thanks,

Iris xx

Made in the USA
Columbia, SC
19 July 2024